MY FIRST
BOOK OF
NURSERY
RHYMES

This edition © Ward Lock Limited
1988

First published in the U.S. in
MCMLXXXVIII by Ideals Publishing
Corporation, Nashville, Tennessee.

ISBN 0-8249-8267-3

Printed and bound in Italy

LITTLE MISS MUFFET

Little Miss Muffet
Sat on a tuffet,
Eating her curds and whey.
There came a big spider,
Who sat down beside her
And frightened Miss Muffet away.

MY FIRST
BOOK OF
NURSERY
RHYMES

Illustrated by Margaret Tarrant

IDEALS CHILDREN'S BOOKS
Nashville, Tennessee

OLD MOTHER HUBBARD

Old Mother Hubbard,
Went to the cupboard,
To fetch her poor dog a bone.
But when she got there,
The cupboard was bare,
And so the poor dog had none.

The dame made a curtsey,
The dog made a bow.
The dame said, "Your servant,"
The dog said, "Bow-wow."

6

JACK AND JILL

Jack and Jill went up the hill
To fetch a pail of water.
Jack fell down and broke his crown
And Jill came tumbling after.

Up Jack got and home did trot
As fast as he could caper.
He went to bed and wrapped his head
In vinegar and brown paper.

SING A SONG OF SIXPENCE

Sing a song of sixpence,
A pocket full of rye.
Four and twenty blackbirds,
Baked in a pie!

When the pie was opened,
The birds began to sing.
Wasn't that a dainty dish,
To set before the king?

The king was in his counting house,
Counting out his money.
The queen was in the parlour,
Eating bread and honey.

The maid was in the garden,
Hanging out the clothes,
When down came a blackbird
And pecked off her nose!

LITTLE BO-PEEP

Little Bo-peep has lost her sheep,
And doesn't know where to find them.
Leave them alone, and they'll come home,
Wagging their tails behind them.

HUMPTY DUMPTY

Humpty Dumpty sat on the wall,
Humpty Dumpty had a great fall.
All the king's horses and all the king's men,
Couldn't put Humpty together again!

BAA, BAA, BLACK SHEEP

Baa, baa, black sheep,
Have you any wool?

Yes Sir, yes Sir,
Three bags full.

One for my master,
And one for my dame.

And one for the little boy
Who lives down the lane.

WHERE ARE YOU GOING?

"Where are you going, my pretty maid?"
"I'm going a-milking, Sir," she said,
"Sir," she said, "Sir," she said.
"I'm going a-milking, Sir," she said.

"What is your fortune, my pretty maid?"
"My face is my fortune, Sir," she said,
"Sir," she said, "Sir," she said.
"My face is my fortune, Sir," she said.

"Then I can't marry you, my pretty maid."
"Nobody asked you, Sir," she said.
"Sir," she said, "Sir," she said.
"Nobody asked you, Sir," she said.

OLD KING COLE

Old King Cole
Was a merry old soul,
And a merry old soul was he.
He called for his pipe,
And he called for his bowl,
And he called for his fiddlers three.

PEASE PORRIDGE HOT

Pease porridge hot,
Pease porridge cold,
Pease porridge in the pot
Nine days old.

Some like it hot,
Some like it cold,
Some like it in the pot
Nine days old.

JACK SPRAT

Jack Sprat could eat no fat,
His wife could eat no lean,
And so between them both, you see,
They licked the platter clean.

RUB-A-DUB-DUB

Rub-a-dub-dub,
Three men in a tub,
And how do you think they got there?
The butcher, the baker,
The candlestick maker,
They all jumped out of a rotten potato,
'Twas enough to make a man stare.

RIDE A COCK HORSE

Ride a cock horse to Banbury Cross,
To see a fine lady upon a white horse.
With rings on her fingers,
And bells on her toes,
She shall have music wherever she goes.

LITTLE TOMMY TUCKER

Little Tommy Tucker
Sings for his supper.
What shall we give him?
Brown bread and butter.
How will he cut it
Without a knife?
How can he marry
Without e'er a wife?

DING DONG BELL

Ding dong bell,
Pussy's in the well.
Who put her in?
Little Johnny Green.
Who pulled her out?
Little Tommy Stout.

What a naughty boy was that
To try and drown poor pussy cat,
Who never did any harm,
But killed all the mice
In his father's barn.

BYE, BABY BUNTING

Bye, baby bunting,
Daddy's gone a-hunting,
To get a little rabbit's skin
To wrap his baby bunting in.

LITTLE BOY BLUE

Little Boy Blue
Come blow your horn!
The sheep's in the meadow,
The cow's in the corn!

Where is the boy
Who looks after the sheep?
He's under the haystack
Fast asleep!

Will you wake him?
No, not I,
For if I do,
He's sure to cry.

SIMPLE SIMON

Simple Simon met a pieman
Going to the fair.
Said Simple Simon to the pieman,
"Please let me taste your ware."

Said the pieman to Simple Simon
"Show me first your penny."
Said Simple Simon to the pieman,
"Indeed I have not any."

Simple Simon went a-fishing,
For to catch a whale.
All the water he had got
Was in his mother's pail!

Simple Simon went to look
If plums grew on a thistle.
He pricked his finger very much,
Which made poor Simon whistle!

MARY, MARY, QUITE CONTRARY

Mary, Mary, quite contrary,
How does your garden grow?
With silver bells and cockle shells,
And pretty maids all in a row, row, row,
And pretty maids all in a row.

HEY DIDDLE-DIDDLE

Hey diddle-diddle,
The cat and the fiddle,
The cow jumped over the moon.
The little boy laughed
To see such fun,
And the dish ran away with the spoon!

WEE WILLIE WINKIE

Wee Willie Winkie
Runs through the town,
Upstairs and downstairs,
In his nightgown.

Calling through the window,
Crying through the lock,
"Are all the children in their beds?
It's after eight o'clock!"

HICKORY, DICKORY, DOCK

Hickory, dickory, dock!
The mouse ran up the clock.
The clock struck one,
The mouse ran down,
Hickory, dickory, dock.

GEORGIE PORGIE

Georgie Porgie, pudding and pie,
Kissed the girls and made them cry.
When the boys came out to play,
Georgie Porgie ran away.

TOM, TOM, THE PIPER'S SON

Tom, Tom, the piper's son,
Stole a pig and away did run.
The pig was eat, and Tom was beat,
And Tom went crying down the street.

RING-A-RING O' ROSES

Ring-a-ring o' roses,
A pocket full of posies,
A-tishoo! A-tishoo!
We all fall down.

THIS LITTLE PIG

This little pig went to market,
This little pig stayed at home,
This little pig had roast beef,
But this little pig had none,
And this little pig cried,
"Wee, wee, wee,
All the way home!"

THE QUEEN OF HEARTS

The Queen of Hearts,
She made some tarts,
All on a summer's day.
The Knave of Hearts,
He stole the tarts,
And took them clean away.

The King of Hearts,
Called for the tarts,
And beat the Knave full sore.
The Knave of Hearts
Brought back the tarts,
And vowed he'd steal no more.

HUSH-A-BYE BABY

Hush-a-bye baby,
On the tree top.
When the wind blows,
The cradle will rock.
When the bough breaks
The cradle will fall,
And down will come baby,
Cradle and all.

POLLY, PUT THE KETTLE ON

Polly, put the kettle on,
Polly, put the kettle on,
Polly, put the kettle on,
   We'll all have tea.

Sally, take it off again,
Sally, take it off again,
Sally, take it off again,
They've all gone away.

INDEX OF FIRST LINES